GEORGE O'CONNOR

ARES

BRINGER OF WAR

A NEAL PORTER BOOK

First Second

New York

TO KNOW THE GREAT GOD ARES,
YOU MUST FIRST KNOW HOW HE
DIFFERS FROM ATHENA.

BOTH ARE GODS OF WAR.

ATHENA IS THE GODDESS OF MARTIAL SKILL.

OF FORMATIONS

OF STRATEGY

OF TRAINING REALIZED AND WISDOM APPLIED.

OF THE BEST POSSIBLE DEFENSE BEING THE BEST POSSIBLE OFFENSE.

HE ARRIVES IN A CHARIOT DRIVEN BY HIS SISTER-IN-ARMS, ERIS, THE GODDESS OF STRIFE AND DISCORD.

ARES, WAR INSATIATE. HIS ARMOR BLAZING LIKE FIRE. DEALING DEATH.

HE IS FLANKED BY HIS SONS, DEIMOS AND PHOBOS, FEAR AND PANIC.

THEIR PRESENCE IS TERRIBLE; FOES SCATTER BEFORE THEM.

TO CLIMB ATOP A PILE OF YOUR ENEMIES, TO HOLD OUT YOUR ARMS SOAKED IN GORE—

AND LAUGH. AND REJOICE. AND WANT *MORE.*

THAT... IS ARES.

THESE LAST TEN YEARS, CAMPED OUT BEFORE THE WALLS OF TROY, WE HAVE ALL, GREEK AND TROJAN ALIKE, KNOWN ATHENA AND ARES INTIMATELY.

PERHAPS NO ONE MORE THAN I. MY NAME IS ASKALAPHOS, WHICH MEANS OWL, THE SYMBOL OF LADY ATHENA. AND ARES... ARES IS MY FATHER.

GREETINGS, FATHER, MOTHER.

UNCLE, BROTHERS AND SISTERS.

AND GREETINGS TO YOU, LADY APHRODITE.

HA. CHARMER.

ICK.

TAKES AFTER HIS FATHER—

AND RIGHT IN FRONT OF POOR HEPHAISTOS.

THE COST HAS BEEN HIGH FOR BOTH SIDES.

BUT MUCH THAT IS FATED TO OCCUR HAS NOT HAPPENED YET. WE MAY NEED TO TAKE A MORE ACTIVE HAND.

PLEASE, LORD ZEUS, LET NO HARM COME TO MY SON, ACHILLES. HE IS ONLY A MORTAL, HIS TIME SO SHORT ALREADY...

HM.

WHAT NEWS FROM THE FIELD, ARES?

I WAS... LISTENING TO THE GREEKS.

THEY BELIEVE WE GODS HAVE NO INTEREST IN THIS WAR AGAINST THE TROJANS.

THEY WILL GIVE UP SOON, I THINK.

YOU ARE NOT THE ONLY GOD WITH CHILDREN IN THIS CONFLICT, THETIS.

WE ALL STAND TO LOSE SONS...WELL, ALMOST ALL, RIGHT, ATHENA?

IT'S MY CHOICE TO HAVE NO HUSBAND AND NO CHILDREN.

IF YOU STAND TO LOSE A SON—YOU HAVE NO ONE TO BLAME BUT YOURSELF.

19

28

ARES! THERE YOU ARE!

APOLLO.

WHY ARE YOU, OF ALL GODS, SITTING ON THE SIDELINES?

THIS MORTAL DIOMEDES! HE STABBED THE LADY APHRODITE IN THE WRIST! HE EVEN CAME AFTER ME! YOU MUST DEAL WITH HIM!

HA.

AT LAST...

IT'S ARES! FALL BACK!

HOW MANY HAVE FALLEN BEFORE HEKTOR AND ARES?

HOW MANY HAVE BEEN SLAUGHTERED?!

BRAVE TEUTHRAS.

MIGHTY ORESTES.

NOBLE TRECHOS.

SHINING HELENOS.

THE CHANCE AT AN END TO THE WAR SNATCHED AWAY, PATROCLUS, BELOVED OF ACHILLES, HATCHED A PLAN.

HE DONNED THE ARMOR OF FAIR ACHILLES AND RALLIED THE GREEKS.

THE FIGHTING SPIRIT OF THE GREEKS SWELLED; THEY THOUGHT THAT THEIR MIGHTY ACHILLES HAD RETURNED.

THE TROJANS WERE SIMILARLY TERRIFIED, FOR THEY DID NOT KNOW THAT THIS WAS AN IMPOSTOR, THAT THE REAL ACHILLES WAS STILL SAFE IN HIS SHIP.

UNTIL POOR PATROCLUS CAME UP AGAINST FEARSOME HEKTOR, AND WAS SLAIN.

UH-OH.

UH—

YOU THOUGHT YOU WERE A MATCH FOR ME?

STICK TO HUNTING DEER.

HE WOULDN'T—

HE COULDN'T!

OH, ACHILLES—

THIS... THIS IS BARBARIC.

WITHOUT A PROPER BURIAL, WITHOUT A COIN IN HIS MOUTH, I WON'T BE ABLE TO ESCORT HEKTOR TO THE OTHER SIDE.

HEKTOR WAS A NOBLE FOE—HE DESERVES BETTER THAN THIS.

A SPELL, TO PROTECT HIS BODY FROM CORRUPTION.

THE FIGHTING
CONTINUED...

BUT THE WHOLE ENDEAVOR
WAS SOURED.

ONE BY ONE, THE
OLYMPIANS LOST INTEREST.

LITTLE BY LITTLE,
THEY DRIFTED AWAY.

UNTIL NONE REMAINED.

EXCEPT YOU.

EXCEPT ME.

I AM GOD OF WAR, BUT NOT OF STRATEGY. STRATEGY IS ATHENA'S DOMAIN.

BUT AS SMART AS SHE IS, FOR ALL HER STRATAGEMS AND INTRIGUES, SHE COULD NEVER SEE THIS.

SHE WHO CHOSE NEVER TO HAVE CHILDREN.

NOT LIKE YOU. NOT LIKE ME.

WE HAVE NOT BEEN THE MOST DEVOTED OF FATHERS, YOU AND I. CHILDREN HAVE ALWAYS CHALLENGED THEIR FATHERS. AND WHO HAS MORE CHILDREN THAN ALMIGHTY ZEUS?

THIS WAR WAS YOUR GAMBIT. TO SET THE GODDESSES AGAINST ONE ANOTHER. TO THIN OUT THE HERD OF DEMIGODS. TO SECURE YOUR POWER.

AUTHOR'S NOTE

I've met a lot of Athenas in my day.

I've also met a handful of Aphrodites, a few Hermeses, and an Apollo and an Artemis or two. Both a Heracles and a Hera. I even met a Zeus, a young guy maybe ten years old.

I make a lot of appearances, at schools, bookstores, and the like, and it's always exciting to meet mythologically named fans. Honestly, I'm a little envious of someone who gets to go through life as a Dionysus or a Persephone. But there is one godly name that I've encountered more than any other—almost as much as every other name combined. Can you guess who?

If you guessed Ares, congratulations (although really, since you're holding his book, it shouldn't be that much of a surprise). Now to be fair, a good number of these Areses whom I've met are actually Aristides, but since that name means "son of Ares" I still count it. Why are so many people naming their baby sons Ares? Don't they know who Ares is? He's described by words like bloodthirsty, violent, man-slaughtering, murderous—words I rarely hear being used to describe a baby. Even his own father didn't like Ares!

When the time came to tell the story of Ares in OLYMPIANS, I thought this would be a good chance to tell the story of the *Iliad*. The *Iliad* is the first of two ancient epic poems attributed to the Greek poet Homer. It's set during the famous Trojan War, and is largely concerned with the Greek demigod Achilles and his wrathful anger. The Olympians appear throughout, watching and scheming from afar, but also getting down and dirty in the proceedings.

With a focus on the gods' role in the Trojan War it only made sense that Ares should step to the fore. One of the themes of the book is a comparison and contrast between Ares and Athena, the other Grecian war deity. Another significant theme that presented itself was the relationship of Ares to his father, Zeus (not good), and Ares himself as a father. A lot of semi-divine offspring meet their end in the *Iliad*, and the only god we see mourn their child is Ares. Violent Ares, bloodthirsty Ares, most-hated-god-on-Olympus Ares . . . is also sensitive father Ares.

Hmm, maybe that's why so many people name their children Aristides.

George O'Connor
Brooklyn, NY
2014

Adapting a very famous epic poem that is 15,693 lines into a sixty-six-page page graphic novel may sound like a job for a lunatic, but . . . well, yeah, I have no comeback for that. In order to make this work, I had to limit the scope of what I showed. For some reason, there have been quite a few retellings of the Iliad that completely omit the gods—Wolfgang Petersen's 2004 movie *Troy*, for example, or Eric Shanower's excellent ongoing comics series *Age of Bronze*—but for me, the godly bits are the most exciting part.

ARES
GOD OF WAR

GOD OF War (the destructive, frenzied side of it)

ROMAN NAME Mars

SYMBOLS Spear, Helmet, Sword

SACRED ANIMALS Woodpecker, Vulture, Dog, Rooster

SACRED PLACES Thrace (site of his birth and center of his cult), Sparta (most warlike of the Greek nations), the Areopagus ("rock of Ares," a hill in Athens where criminal trials were held)

DAY OF THE WEEK Tuesday

MONTH March

HEAVENLY BODY The planet Mars

MODERN LEGACY The rockets designed to carry the next generation of space vehicles into orbit are called Ares, after the god.

The word "martial," as in martial arts, is derived from Ares's Roman name, Mars. It means, appropriately, "warlike."

♂, the gender symbol for men, is a representation of Ares's spear and shield.

GₐREEK NOTES

PAGES 4–5: Intro our hero. This was a fun spread to draw, and that's no lie.

PAGE 6 PANEL 1: Speaking of fun, I was super excited to get a chance to draw Eris, goddess of troublemaking again—she ended up being my favorite part of the previous volume of OLYMPIANS, *Aphrodite: Goddess of Love*. I was so enamored of the character of Eris that in the early stages of *Ares* I spent a while trying to install her as narrator. That was a bad idea because (a) she hardly appears in the *Iliad*, the epic poem by Homer that provides the framework for this book, and (b) since she's crazier than an outhouse rat she makes for a spectacularly unreliable narrator.

PAGE 6 PANEL 4: Deimos and Phobos are more personified abstracts concepts than actual gods, hence their spooky wraithlike appearances.

PAGE 8 PANEL 4: At multiple times in the *Iliad*, Ares is referred to as "blood-dripping," as if he's always coated in other people's blood. Pretty gross.

PAGE 9 PANEL 2: Ares's son Askalaphos is not the same dude as Askalaphos the gardener of Hades, whom we met on page 51 of *Hades: Lord of the Dead*. I guess in ancient Greece "owl" was a pretty popular name. Also note he calls himself Greek—strictly speaking that's inaccurate. The *Iliad* predates the word Greek. They would have called themselves either Achaians or Danaans. I just used Greek because it's more familiar to our ears.

PAGE 10: It may seem like I'm dropping you in the middle of the action, but this is pretty much exactly where the *Iliad* begins. People tend to think of it as the story of the Trojan War, but it really covers only a few weeks in the war's tenth year, and doesn't even go to the end.

PAGE 11: Iris, in addition to being the goddess of the rainbow, is the messenger of the gods when Hermes is busy. Considering all the stuff that guy has to do I'm surprised we don't see more of her.

PAGES 12–13 PANEL 1: Here we see the assembled dramatis personae of Mount Olympus for this story—a different assemblage than we normally see in most myths. From left to right, we have Ares, Iris, Aphrodite, Poseidon, Leto, Apollo, Artemis, Hephaistos, Athena, Hera, Hermes, Zeus, and Thetis. The addition of Thetis makes sense, as her son Achilles is the crux of so much of the story of the *Iliad*. Leto, mother of Artemis and Apollo, is a more curious addition to the proceedings, especially given her longstanding enmity with Hera (as seen very briefly in OLYMPIANS Book 3, *Hera: The Goddess and Her Glory*). Noticeably absent are Demeter, Hestia, and Dionysos, though all three are mentioned in the *Iliad*. Hades, not a true Olympian, makes his unseen presence felt elsewhere in the story.

PAGE 14 PANELS 1 AND 2: Flashback courtesy of OLYMPIANS Book 6, *Aphrodite: Goddess of Love*.

PAGE 15 PANEL 3: That's Priam, king of Troy, and Helen, the most beautiful woman in the world watching from the ramparts.

PAGE 20: Remember what I said a few comments ago about how Hades makes his unseen presence felt elsewhere? Get it? It's his helmet of invisibility! SEE HOW FUNNY I AM? Hermes, of course, is dispatched to get it because he's the only Olympian who can freely enter the Underworld. Athena needs it because the helmet makes its wearer invisible, even to other gods.

PAGE 22 PANELS 1–3: Cameos by a few of the greatest heroes of the Trojan War. High King Agamemnon (who we first met a few pages ago), Ajax, the strongest of the Greeks (who is best known today for lending his name to the scouring cleanser), and Odysseus, eponymous star of the *Odyssey* and whom we first met in Olympians Book 5, *Poseidon: Earth Shaker.*

PAGE 25: Diomedes, the King of Argos, is not to be confused with the Diomedes of Thrace, who was fed to his own man-eating horses by Heracles on page 45 of Olympians Book 3, *Hera: The Goddess and Her Glory.* Apparently Diomedes and Askalaphos were the Michael and Jacob of their day.

PAGE 27 PANEL 1: Elysium being the paradise where you went after you died if you were "lucky" enough to die valiantly in battle.

PAGE 28 PANEL 6: Apollo is an oracular god, so he would know. After the fall of Troy, Aeneas goes on to found what will eventually become Rome. That's a pretty important fate, I suppose.

PAGE 31 PANEL 1: Intro of Prince Hektor, older brother of Paris and next in line for the throne of Troy after Priam. Hektor is a pretty fascinating character, being arguably the most noble and sympathetic character in the *Iliad,* and he's a Trojan, ostensibly the bad guys.

PAGE 32 PANEL 1: The *Iliad* describes how Ares is everywhere among the Trojans, and how "he ranged now in front of Hektor, and now behind him" in the "likeness of a man mortal." I chose to depict this as multiple, um, Areses, swarming all over the Greek battlements. We are seeing this scene from Diomedes's enchanted eyes, but to the average participant it would look like a crowd of ordinary Trojans. Whether Ares had split himself into multiple incarnations or whether he was moving so fast as to appear in several places at once I leave to you, the reader, to decide.

PAGE 33: The word *stentorian,* an adjective describing a person's voice as "loud and powerful," enters our vernacular from Hera's impersonation here.

PAGE 33 PANEL 9: The *Iliad* specifically mentions that the oaken axle of the chariot groans in protest when Athena steps on it. It's a cool little detail, that gods weigh more than mortals, that my geeky, growing-up-reading-the-official-handbook-of-the-Marvel-Universe self loves.

PAGE 36 PANEL 3: One of my favorite lines from the *Iliad.* To quote Lattimore's translation: "Then Ares the brazen bellowed with a sound as great as nine thousand men make, or ten thousand."

PAGE 37 PANEL 2: Previous recordholder was Heracles, who in various tellings wounded various Olympians, but never two in one day. Take that, Heracles!

PAGE 38: Even though he's known as blood-dripping Ares, that gold stuff isn't blood. The immortal Olympians had a substance called ichor coursing through their veins.

PAGE 41 PANEL 5: It says a lot about Ares that even though his son was Greek, and was killed by a Trojan, that he's going to exact revenge on the Greeks.

PAGE 43 PANEL 1: The composition of this panel is an homage to one of my favorite paintings *Jupiter and Thetis,* by Jean Auguste Dominique Ingres. Check it out—Jupiter (Zeus) couldn't look more diesel. The incident with the hekatoncheires can be seen in Olympians Book 5, *Poseidon: Earth Shaker.*

PAGE 44 PANEL 4: And this is a tale for another day.

PAGE 46: In some later stories, Thetis made Achilles invincible by dipping him in the River Styx. His only vulnerable spot was his heel, which was where she held him as she dunked him. In Homer's *Iliad*, no mention is made of this supposed invincibility—in fact, in Book 21, an ambidextrous Trojan named Asteropaios throws two spears at him at once and actually draws blood on Achilles' arm. I figure though, any demigod wearing a set of custom armor forged by Hephaistos himself is gonna be plenty hard enough to kill even without being absolutely invincible.

PAGE 46: Achilles is the king of the Myrmidons, a legendary group of people whose name meant "ant-people." To that effect I based elements of his Hephaistos-designed armor on ants.

PAGE 50: Moral of the story is: don't mestus with Hephaistos.

PAGE 52–53: GOD ON GOD ACTION! CAN YOU FEEL THE EXCITEMENT? This sequence is the mythological equivalent of when the Avengers bump into the X-Men. They're both on the same side, but you know when they meet that there'll be a misunderstanding or something that will result in Thor punching Wolverine into orbit or some other similarly awesome event.

PAGE 58 PANEL 5: I'm pretty sure that this is the only punch that's been thrown in the whole series.

PAGE 61: Achilles's mistreatment of the body of Hektor was a huge cultural no-no and was a big part of the reason the gods were so upset with the Greeks after the war.

PAGE 63–64: Contrary to popular belief, The Iliad does not conclude with the end of the Trojan War, but rather with the funeral of Hektor after Hermes is successful in aiding Priam at reclaiming his son's body from Achilles. Provided for your edification, here are the descriptions of the remaining beats of the war depicted in the illustrations.

PAGE 63 PANEL 2: The death of the Amazon Queen Penthesilea, a Trojan ally and the daughter of Ares, at the hands of Achilles.

PAGE 63 PANEL 4: Achilles meets his end from an arrow in the heel fired by Paris, the source of the expression Achilles heel.

PAGE 64 PANEL 1: The Trojan horse. The Greeks pretended to retreat, and presented to the Trojans a giant wooden horse as a sort of goodbye gift. In actuality, it was secretly filled with Greek soldiers. After it was brought into Troy, they snuck out at night and sacked and burned the city. Source of the expression "Trojan horse" and "beware of Greeks bearing gifts," it was seen briefly before in OLYMPIANS Book 5, *Poseidon: Earth Shaker*. Cassandra, sister of Hektor and Paris who was gifted with the power of prophecy and cursed that no one would believe her, begs futilely for the horse not to be brought into Troy.

PAGE 64 PANEL 3: The sack of Troy. In the foreground, King Priam is being clubbed to death by Neoptolemos, the son of Achilles. In the background, in what is surely the most disturbing incident in all of Greek mythology, Greek soldiers throw Hektor's infant son Astyanax off the walls of Troy.

PAGE 64 PANEL 5: Aeneas escapes Troy, with his father, son, and the Palladium, a wooden statue of Athena that was meant to protect the city. As already noted, Aeneas founds what will eventually become Rome in Italy. His story is told in the Roman epic poem the *Aeneid*. The Palladium remained for years in Rome, housed in the temple of Vesta. Supposedly it was transferred out of Rome to Constantinople by Constantine and is now lost.

PAGE 66 PANEL 6: Zing! And that's the end of another installment of G(r)eek Notes. See you all next time.

ABOUT THIS BOOK

ARES: BRINGER OF WAR is the seventh book in OLYMPIANS, a graphic novel series from First Second that retells the Greek myths.

FOR DISCUSSION

1 Who do you like better, Ares or Athena? Who would you rather meet? Who do you think you are more similar to?

2 Why do you think that Zeus dislikes Ares so much? Was it nice to say those things in front of everybody?

3 The gods get in a big fight with one another in this book. Who are some of the gods that you would like to see fight each other?

4 How many soldiers are in this book? You should totally count them (don't really, you'll go crazy).

5 Where do you think Demeter, Hestia, and Dionysos were during this book?

6 This is the first volume of OLYMPIANS in which that tricky George didn't sneak in the line "Mount Olympus, the tallest mountain left standing." What do you think about that?

7 Ares is arguably the most handsome of the gods, but also arguably the most violent. Why do you think that is?

8 Very few people believe in the Greek gods today. Why do you think it is important that we still learn about them?

ERIS

TROUBLEMAKER OF THE GODS

GODDESS OF Strife, Discord, Arguments

ALSO KNOWN AS Enyo

ROMAN NAME Discordia

SYMBOL Apple of Discord

HEAVENLY BODY The dwarf planet Eris

MODERN LEGACY There is a genus of jumping spiders which, while not poisonous or particularly big, are very bitey and terrifying-looking, and so are appropriately named after Eris.

BIBLIOGRAPHY

HOMER. THE ILIAD, TRANSLATED BY RICHMOND LATTIMORE.
UNIVERSITY OF CHICAGO PRESS, 1951.

Ares: Bringer of War is unusual in the OLYMPIANS series because its source material was primarily this single book. There are many translations of the *Iliad* available, but I used this one as it's widely held that Lattimore's does the best job of preserving the flavor of the ancient Greek. Consequently, however, it was a bit of a slog. I had previously read the Robert Fagles version; that one might be said to have a little more pizzazz going on, language-wise.

THEOI GREEK MYTHOLOGY WEB SITE   WWW.THEOI.COM

An online archive of hundreds of ancient Greek and Roman texts. Many of these have never been published in the traditional sense, and many are just fragments recovered from ancient papyrus, or recovered text from other authors' quotations of lost epics. Invaluable.

MYTH INDEX WEB SITE   WWW.MYTHINDEX.COM

Another mythology Web site connected to Theoi.com. While it doesn't have the painstakingly compiled quotations from ancient texts, it does offer some impressive encyclopedic entries on virtually every character to ever pass through a Greek myth. Pretty amazing.

ALSO RECOMMENDED
FOR YOUNGER READERS

D'Aulaires' Book of Greek Myths. Ingri and Edgar Parin D'Aulaire. New York: Doubleday, 1962.

Black Ships Before Troy. Rosemary Sutcliff and Alan Lee. London: Francis Lincoln, 2005.

FOR OLDER READERS

The Marriage of Cadmus and Harmony. Robert Calasso. New York: Knopf, 1993.

Mythology. Edith Hamilton. New York: Grand Central Publishing, 1999.

The Lost Books of the Odyssey. Zachary Mason. New York: Farrar, Strauss and Giroux, 2010.

The Age of Bronze. Graphic novel series. Eric Shanower. Berkley, CA: Image Comics, 2001.

ACHILLES

GREATEST WARRIOR OF THE TROJAN WAR

HEAVENLY BODY 588 Achilles, the first asteroid discovered

MODERN LEGACY Named in reference to the injury to the heel that brought down this nigh-invulnerable Greek hero, the tendon that runs down the back of your leg is called the Achilles tendon.

Similarly, any weakness in an otherwise impregnable object is called an Achilles heel.

To all those who have ever fought the good fight
—G.O.

:01

First Second

New York

Copyright © 2015 by George O'Connor

Published by First Second
First Second is an imprint of Roaring Brook Press,
a division of Holtzbrinck Publishing Holdings Limited Partnership
175 Fifth Avenue, New York, NY 10010

Library of Congress Cataloging-in-Publication Data

O'Connor, George.
Ares : bringer of war / George O'Connor. — First edition.
pages cm. — (Olympians ; 7)
"A Neal Porter Book."
Summary: "The myth continues in the tenth year of the fabled Trojan War where two infamous gods of war go to battle"— Provided by publisher.
ISBN 978-1-62672-013-8 (paperback)
ISBN 978-1-62672-014-5 (paper over board)
1. Ares (Greek deity)—Juvenile literature. 2. Trojan War—Juvenile literature. 3. Ares (Greek deity)—Comic books, strips, etc. 4. Trojan War—Comic books, strips, etc. I. Title.
BL820.M2O26 2014
741.5'973—dc23

2014041225

First Second books may be purchased for business or promotional use.
For information on bulk purchases please contact Macmillan Corporate
and Premium Sales Department at (800) 221-7945 x5442 or by email at
specialmarkets@macmillan.com.

FIRST

EDITION

First Edition 2015

Cover design by Colleen AF Venable
Book design by Rob Steen

Printed in China by Toppan Leefung Printing Ltd., Dongguan City, Guangdong Province

Paperback: 10 9
Hardcover: 10 9 8 7 6 5